PARADISE HOUSE

The Zoo
in the ATTIC

PARADISE HOUSE

The Zoo in the ATTIC

HILARY McKAY

Hodder
Children's
Books

a division of Hodder Headline plc

First published in Great Britain in 1995
by Victor Gollancz

The edition first published in 1998
by Hodder Children's Books

10 9 8 7 6 5 4 3 2 1

A Catalogue record for this book is
available from the British Library

ISBN 0 340 72286 X

Offset by Hewer Text Ltd, Edinburgh

Printed and bound in Great Britain by
Mackays of Chatham plc, Chatham

Hodder Children's Books
A Division of Hodder Headline plc
338 Euston Road
London NW1 3BH

PARADISE HOUSE

The Zoo in the ATTIC

Chapter One

At school they were known as the angels from Paradise House. People said, "Grown wings yet?" and "Show us your halo!" but the children, Danny, Nathan and Anna, did not care. They liked living in Paradise House and they were never in any real danger of being mistaken for anything heavenly.

Paradise House was a large, square, red-brick building, more than a hundred years old. It was in London, not quite in the middle but, "Nearer to the middle than the edges," said Nathan when his father (who was a bus driver) brought home a map of the city to show the children exactly where they lived.

"Handy for the zoo," added Danny O'Brien, looking affectionately at the patch of green that was Regent's Park. Danny was well known for his love of animals and the zoo was his favourite place in the world.

Once Paradise House had been the home of a rich family. It had a basement (rather dark and gloomy) where the servants had worked, a ground floor (extremely posh) where the family had lived, a first floor (still very posh) where the family had slept, and a second floor (not at all posh) where the children had their nursery and where the servants had slept when they were not working. Across the top of the whole of the house was an enormous attic.

Since those good old days (if you were family), or bad old days (if you were servants), everything had changed. The house had been divided up into flats, each with two, three or four rooms, and all sorts of people lived in them. The bright elaborate rooms downstairs had grown much plainer and the plain rooms at the top of the house had become slightly brighter. Only the attic was unchanged. The attic was, and always had been, full of spiders.

Danny O'Brien and his mother had a flat right at the top, under the attic. They lived where the children would have lived in the past. Danny's bedroom still had the bars at the window that showed it had once been a nursery. Danny was fond of the bars; they reminded him of the zoo.

Anna Lee and her parents lived underneath Danny and his mother. Her family were Chinese, and Nathan Amadi's family, who lived in the flat below Anna's, had come to London years before from Nigeria in Africa. Although both families had lived in England for a long time, it did not stop the children from hoping that one day some relations of Nathan's or Anna's would arrive suddenly at Paradise House and invite them all back home for the school holidays.

Danny and Anna and Nathan were all in the same class at school. Out of school they spent so much time clattering up and down the staircase visiting each other that their parents hardly ever knew exactly where they were.

"Very useful sometimes," remarked

Anna, and Danny and Nathan agreed.

There were other people living in Paradise House as well. A rather bad-tempered caretaker, Mr McDonald (but the children always called him Old McDonald), lurked in the basement, and two old ladies, known as the Miss Kents, shared the ground-floor flat opposite Nathan's. The Miss Kents had lived in Paradise House for years and years but Old McDonald had lived there for ever. He was the only person who remembered Paradise House before it had been turned into flats. His father had worked for the people who had owned it then, and Old McDonald had been "born in the basement" as he was fond of telling everyone.

Even with all these people living in Paradise House there were still empty rooms left over.

"I wish somebody useful would move in," said Danny one day.

"What sort of useful?" asked Anna.

"A zoo-keeper perhaps," said Danny. "The sort of zoo-keeper that sometimes has to take the animals home."

"*Are* there such people?" asked Anna doubtfully.

"Or a policeman with Alsatians. Or a mounted policeman with a horse."

"I'm sure they don't take the horses home," said Anna.

"Or a petshop owner. Or just someone with lots of dogs and cats."

"The Miss Kents downstairs had a canary," said Anna, "but it died. So they thought they might like a parrot instead and they went and asked about the one in the petshop down the road . . . "

"William?" interrupted Danny, who knew the petshop well.

"Yes, William," said Anna. "But they didn't buy him."

"Good!" said Danny. "If I get enough birthday money next week I might buy William myself."

"You won't," said Anna certainly. "He costs six hundred pounds!"

"*Six hundred pounds!*" repeated Danny.

"That's why they didn't buy him," explained Anna.

"They could buy a whole zoo for six hundred pounds," Danny remarked.

"They wouldn't want a whole zoo," said Anna. "Where would anyone put a whole zoo?"

"I'm sure I could think of somewhere," said Danny.

The day before Danny's ninth birthday his mother got him out of bed and under the shower and into his clothes and through his breakfast, all before he had time to wake up enough to protest. Then she made him take everything he could carry from his bedroom and dump it into hers.

"Why?" asked Danny, staggering sleepily past her beneath a load of animal books.

"Secret," said Danny's mother and she collected up an armful of soft toys, plastic zoo models and Danny's life-size crocodile pyjama case.

"Is it something to do with my birthday?"

"Perhaps," said Danny's mother.

"Do you know what you're getting me yet?"

"Of course." Danny's mother fished under the bed where Danny kept his Natural History Museum and came out with something horrible in a jam-jar.

"What's this disgusting-looking stuff?" she demanded.

"Swamp water," said Danny.

"What on earth is swamp water?"

"Secret recipe," said Danny rescuing the jar, together with a pair of stag's antlers, an old bird's nest and a box of dead flies and bees that he had collected in the park. "It's the same sort of stuff that dinosaurs used to live in, except they had ferns instead of lettuce. Have you got my birthday present yet?"

"Of course I have," said his mother. "It was ordered weeks ago!"

Danny brightened up tremendously and hurried away to cart out his Noah's ark quilt, his conger-eel lamp and his dinosaur footprint bedside rug. When he returned for the next load his mother was taking posters off the wall.

"Why are you taking them down?"

demanded Danny.

"You'll see tomorrow," replied his mother.

"I wish I knew what you were getting me," said Danny, and he made the same remark about forty times during the next half-hour until his mother finally lost her temper.

"School!" she ordered.

"I haven't finished my breakfast properly!" protested Danny. "I didn't have any toast!"

His mother chopped two slices off a loaf of bread and rammed them into the toaster. While she waited for them to toast Danny passed the time by saying, "I wonder what you've got me. I wonder what you've got me," very quietly to himself and over and over again.

"Danny," said his mother warningly.

"I only wondered," said Danny, "in case I ought to get ready for it. Buy dog biscuits or something."

His mother ignored this enormous hint.

"I wish I knew," said Danny. "I wish I

knew I wish I knew I wish I . . . "

"Wallpaper!" shouted Danny's mother and the kitchen filled up with black smoke.

"What?"

"Wallpaper, wallpaper, wallpaper! Oh bother! The toaster has jammed! You'll have to have bread!"

"You *can't* be getting me wallpaper," said

Danny, very shocked. "Wallpaper's not a present!"

'I am and I can and it is, and I'm sticking it up today, and Penny from work is coming to paint the woodwork. It will be ready for your party tomorrow, and, by the way, I've invited Anna."

"I don't want wallpaper! And I'm not inviting girls!"

"You will want this wallpaper," said his mother. "And we're not leaving Anna out when she lives right underneath us. It wouldn't be fair. And, anyway, you went to Anna's party."

Danny stopped protesting about Anna. He didn't mind her coming. He would have invited her himself if he had thought of inviting girls. Instead, he returned to the far more important subject of his birthday.

"What else are you getting me besides wallpaper?"

"Nothing," said Danny's mother.

"Is it a joke?"

"Nope!"

"What about what I asked for?"

"Danny," said his mother. "You are being rude and ridiculous and annoying!"

"It *can't* be wallpaper!" Danny protested. "You couldn't be so horrible!"

"Oh, couldn't I?" replied his mother. "You are wrong! School!" And she kissed him by force and bundled him out of the door.

It was so late when Danny finally arrived at school that there was no one about to listen to his amazingly awful bad news. Everyone was in assembly and Danny sneaked in at the back and sat in a state of explosion until the final notices were read and they were all sent back to their classrooms.

"Right then," said Mr Harper, Danny's class teacher. "Five minutes' gossip and then we'll start work! Who's got some good news to tell us?"

Nobody moved.

"Ordinary news?"

Nobody moved.

"Terrible news?"

Two hands shot up. Nathan beat Danny by a split second. Nathan had received astonishing news the evening before. His eyes were still round with shock.

"My mum's having a baby!" he announced.

"Very nice," said Mr Harper. "Not terrible news at all!"

Nathan gazed at him as if he was mad.

"P'raps she's having twins," suggested Arun Patel wickedly. "My mum did!"

"Twins!" exclaimed Nathan, appalled.

"'S' what mine did," said Arun. "Two at once!"

"Arun!" said Mr Harper warningly. "Let's just get Nathan used to the idea of one baby, shall we? Who else had a hand up? Yes, Danny?"

Danny, who was bursting with impatience, bounced up from his chair and announced: "I've found out what I'm getting for my birthday!"

"Is it what you asked for?" enquired Anna eagerly.

There was no one in Danny's class who did not know what he had requested for his birthday. He had asked for a sheep-dog. If that could not be managed, then an ordinary dog would do, or even a cat. Anything, in fact, that was alive and was not a plant.

Everyone also knew that Danny and his mother lived in a small flat, and that he might as well have dreamed of owning a string of camels as a sheep-dog for all the chance he had of getting either. Only the optimistic Anna had believed that his dream might come true.

"Come on then, Danny!" said Mr Harper. "Spit it out before we burst with curiosity!"

"Wallpaper," said Danny.

There was a moment of horrified silence and then Danny's friends hastened to comfort him.

"I got a set of maths books once," volunteered Anna.

"My gran gave me zip-up slippers for Christmas," said Nathan.

"*My* gran knitted me a Postman Pat jumper," said Peter. "Pale blue, too, and she knitted it big to last. It's got Postman Pat on it, drivin' underneath a rainbow!"

"*I* got a poisonous pork pie for my

birthday not so long ago," added Mr Harper. "And I ate it! There's much worse things than wallpaper, Danny! Especially if someone else sticks it up for you."

"She's sticking it up today," said Danny. "Her and her friend who works at the hairdresser's with her. They've taken a day off."

"Well then," said Mr Harper, and everyone seemed to think that settled it. Danny was getting wallpaper for his birthday, but his friends had known presents nearly as bad. Nathan's mother was having a baby, Arun's mother had had twins and Arun had survived the calamity. Even Mr Harper had once consumed a poisonous pork pie. Life was tough sometimes.

"Tables test!" said Mr Harper.

Life was very tough.

Chapter Two

"Perhaps the wallpaper was just a joke," said Anna, as she walked back from school with Danny that afternoon, but the minute they climbed the steps to the porch they knew that it was true. Paradise House was a great place for smells. They travelled through the house on invisible highways. An unemptied dustbin in the basement reeked in the attic. Curries cooked on the top floor were still fragrant in the hall. As Danny and Anna pushed open the front door, the smell of fresh paint and decorating came rolling and bowling down the stairs to meet them.

"'S'true all right," said Danny as they passed the doorway of Nathan's flat and began to climb the stairs. "I can smell it!"

Anna sighed. She could smell it as well.

At the top of the stairs, she paused at her own front door and gazed worriedly at Danny.

"Shall I come with you?" she asked.

"I'd rather be on my own," said Danny dismally. "I s'pose you'll see it at the party tomorrow."

"S'pose I will," agreed Anna. Her own birthday party, with real Chinese food and paper kites flown in the park, had been such a spectacular success that she was almost ashamed to remember it.

The smell of decorating was now so strong that Danny found his eyes were pricking and blinking. It must have had the same effect on Anna, because as he turned to climb the final flight of stairs he saw two, large, round tears run down her cheeks.

"Danny, don't sulk!" said his gran. She had come to help with the wallpaper cleaning up and stayed to supper afterwards.

"I'm not," said Danny.

"You're your father all over again sometimes," continued Gran cheerfully. "He was a great one for sulking before he Went Off!"

"He wasn't," said Danny. Not that he could remember his father, who had Gone Off, as Gran put it, when Danny was only a few months old.

"Leave him alone!" said Danny's mother. "He's not sulking, he's thinking."

"*You* were a dreadful sulker too," Gran told her. "And cheeky! You still *are* cheeky! Aren't you going to go and look at your room, Danny?"

"It's not my birthday yet," said Danny, not pausing in his awful thinking.

"You'll have to look at bedtime," pointed out Gran.

"I won't," said Danny and at bedtime he closed his eyes tight at the bedroom door, groped across the room to his bed, fumbled his way into his pyjamas and burrowed under the quilt, all without a glance at his bedroom walls. In the darkness, under the quilt, his thoughts were even gloomier, and sometimes he rubbed his eyes and sniffed.

"Danny," said his mother, coming in some time later, "we couldn't possibly keep a sheep-dog!"

"We could," said Danny, very muffled because of the quilt. "It would sleep on my bed."

"What would it do here alone all day?"

"It could play in the attic," said Danny, who had thought that one out long ago.

"All alone with the spiders?"

"Well, we could get two, then," said Danny, almost coming out of the quilt with cheerfulness. "They could play together!"

"Impossible," said Danny's mother, so Danny crawled even further down the bed and thought harder than ever until he fell asleep. And, all of a sudden, it was morning and for the first time he saw his birthday present.

Danny knew then why his mother had so recklessly bought the wallpaper and stuck it up, regardless of his feelings. It could have been made for no one but him.

The whole room was covered in animals. From floor to ceiling were parrots and elephants and lions and bears. There was not a

single gap between them. Every animal that Danny had ever heard of crowded his bedroom walls. Fish, birds, butterflies and beetles filled the small places between beasts of every description. Hundreds of pairs of paper eyes watched Danny wake up.

"There!" said Danny's mother triumphantly from the doorway. "*Now* do you like wallpaper for your birthday?"

"'Course I do!" said Danny valiantly. "It's brilliant!" And he looked bravely at the flat silent paper animals and tried not to think of his sheep-dog.

Of course Danny received other presents as well, including a kit to build a dinosaur skeleton from his aunt, and a fat envelope from Gran containing seven tickets for the zoo, one for each party guest and one for Danny's mother. It was clear that Danny's relations had done their very best to choose presents that were as close to live animals as possible.

The visit to the zoo was a great success

with Danny's guests.

"Come and see my fantastic elephants!" said Nathan.

"Why yours?" asked Danny, feeling very strongly that since it was his birthday party any unclaimed animals should belong to him.

Nathan pointed proudly to the notice that read "African Elephants", and Arun immediately joined in the spotting game and quickly helped himself to all of the tigers and most of the monkeys.

"It's not fair!" complained Danny. "You've never even been to India!"

Arun took no notice and bagged a large herd of deer. Nathan added several giraffes and at least a dozen zebras to his collection, and Robert and Craig thankfully remembered that they had a Scottish grandmother and after a short search found and seized three golden eagles.

"They were *my* birthday tickets!" protested Danny crossly. "What about me?"

"Pigeons," said Arun.

"I don't want pigeons!"

"Wolves?" suggested Anna kindly.

"There aren't any wolves in England!" said Robert and Craig immediately. "There aren't any proper animals in England at all! Nothing good enough to put in a zoo, anyway!"

"I think it's a rotten game, then," said Anna, but even so, when they came to the giant panda, she could not resist joining in. She stood by the cage and smirked and smirked, and could not be persuaded to leave until it was time to go home for the birthday tea. By then Danny was showing signs of starting some more of his thinking, that looked so much like sulking.

"You can share the panda if you like," offered Anna as they left.

"Thanks," said Danny gloomily.

"*I've* got you a proper present," said Anna.

"Thanks," said Danny again and then, remembering, "No, you haven't. You didn't bring anything."

"Mum said to leave him until we got home," explained Anna.

"Him?" asked Danny, amazed.

"Yes," said Anna proudly, and when they arrived back at Paradise House she produced her present.

"His name is Oscar," she told Danny. "I know he's not a sheep-dog, but he's properly alive!"

"He's beautiful!" said Danny, overwhelmed. Oscar, fat and golden, swimming round and round his goldfish bowl, was beautiful.

Nobody else seemed to think Oscar was very exciting. They admired him politely for a few minutes but much preferred the wallpaper and the enormous birthday tea. Only Danny and Anna really believed that three inches of real, live animal were worth all the pretend ones in the world.

"My father got him for you," said Anna. "And he called him Oscar because he had one called Oscar and it learned to come for food when he called his name. He said to tell you he is a small golden carp and very intelligent."

"You can see he's intelligent," agreed

Danny. "Oscar will be a start."

"Start of what?" asked Anna.

"Something I thought of on the bus home."

"Is that why you wouldn't talk to anyone? I thought you were . . . "

"Well, I wasn't," said Danny. "I was thinking about my zoo in the attic."

"What zoo? What attic?" asked Anna, astonished.

"Shush!" Danny glanced warningly across at his mother as he spoke. He was certain that she would not be pleased at the thought of a zoo above her head.

"Why? What zoo? What attic?" persisted Anna.

"Tell you another day," promised Danny.

At that moment Robert and Craig's father arrived to collect them, and Nathan's mother came up the stairs for Nathan and Arun, who was staying the night with him.

"How are the twins?" Nathan's mother asked Arun.

"I don't know," said Arun after a moment's puzzled thinking. "I haven't looked at them lately."

"Is it chucking out time yet?" asked Anna's father appearing in the doorway. "Happy birthday, Danny! I see she managed to part with Oscar after all! It was a close thing, wasn't it, Anna?"

"Dad!" whispered Anna crossly.

"You came very close to getting a box of Liquorice Allsorts!" continued Anna's father tactlessly.

Danny looked at Oscar in dismay and Oscar looked sternly back at him.

"What about if we share him?" suggested Danny.

It was obviously the right thing to say. Danny's mother stopped glaring at him, Anna's father thumped him approvingly on his back, and Anna sighed with relief.

"She took him to bed with her last night," explained her father.

"He swims faster in the dark," said Anna.

Danny lay in the dark and looked at Oscar. He did swim faster. He flickered like a golden-grey ghost of a goldfish, half invisible. Just then Danny would not have swopped him for an attic full of sheep-dogs.

Chapter Three

The stairs to the attic of Paradise House
went up from a doorway beside Danny's
mother's kitchen. The door was supposed to
be kept locked, but soon after Danny and
his mother moved into their flat they found
a key that fitted the lock. They climbed the
attic stairs to investigate, but there was
nothing at all to see except grey, dusty
boards and the undersides of grey slate tiles
and festoons of heavy grey cobwebs.

Danny's mother, who was not fond of
spiders, had taken one horrified look at the
cobwebs and had never gone into the attic
again. The door was locked and the key was
put back on the hook where it belonged and
Danny's mother almost forgot about the
attic. But Danny did not. Sometimes, when
his mother was out and school was over and

the flat seemed very empty, he took the key from the bathroom door and sneaked up the attic stairs to admire the cobwebs.

"It will make a perfect zoo!" he told Anna the Monday after his birthday party. "There's plenty of light comes through the cracks between the tiles and it's full of animals already!"

"What sort of animals?" asked Anna.

"Spiders," said Danny.

"Oh," said Anna.

"You're not scared of spiders, are you?" asked Danny.

"It depends," said Anna.

"They're much smaller than you."

"They've got more legs, though," said Anna and she clutched Oscar in his bowl very tightly as she followed Danny up the attic stairs.

"Spiders will be a help," said Danny encouragingly. "Two sorts of animals already. Spiders and a golden carp!"

"You can see little lines of sky through the roof!" exclaimed Anna when she arrived. "And what's that noise?"

The noise was the scratchy sound of birds on the roof, but they did not discover this until they had found a tile loose enough to push aside a little. An oblong of blue sky appeared above their heads and there was a rustle of wings.

"Sparrows!" said Danny, very pleased. "Three sorts of animals! Do you like it?"

"I like it better now we've made that gap," said Anna.

"We'll make it bigger and put down bread and the sparrows will come in and be company for Oscar."

"What if they eat the spiders?"

"We've plenty of spiders," said Danny magnificently. "Perhaps rats and mice will come too!"

"I shouldn't mind mice," said Anna.

That was how the zoo began. The sparrows came almost straight away, and their food disappeared so quickly that Danny had great hopes that rats and mice were also beginning to visit. It was surprising how easily they managed to find animals when they looked really hard. Soon there was a shoe-box full of woodlice and several jam-jars full of caterpillars, acquired by a series of swops with Nathan, whose grandfather had an allotment. Nathan also supplied them with holey cabbage leaves as cater-pillar food.

"A penny each!" grumbled Danny. "This one is more hole than leaf!"

"We sometimes get free caterpillars, though!" pointed out Anna, who did not pay the bills. She was very fond of the cater-pillars and was quite distressed when they stopped eating and hung themselves on the sides of their jars and turned brown.

"That's what they're meant to do," explained Danny. "They're turning into butterflies."

"I know, but I wish they wouldn't," said Anna. "I can't tell which is which any more!" After a while, she gave up trying to make friends with the hung-up caterpillars and concentrated on their collection of ants. They had discovered a huge supply of them living under the front doorstep. Old

McDonald waged a constant losing battle against this colony of ants, but there never seemed to be any less of them. It was lucky that there were so many because the zoo ants were continually escaping.

"I brought up sixteen yesterday and they're all gone," remarked Anna one afternoon. "I hope your snails haven't eaten them!"

Danny's six snails were almost as hard to keep confined as the ants. The woodlice were not much better, and neither was the large black beetle that they named Mr-Harper-In-The-Box to distinguish him from Mr Harper, their teacher. Danny and Anna became very busy with their collection, designing escape-proof cages, arranging tiles to give maximum sunlight, writing notices and chopping up cabbages and breadcrumbs in the zoo kitchen. Oscar watched them patiently while they worked, swimming round and round his glass bowl. There never was a goldfish as well loved as Oscar, or as well travelled.

"That poor fish!" said Gran one day. "He

doesn't know whether he's coming or going!"

Sometimes Oscar moved house three times a day.

"Backwards and forwards," said Gran. "You'll drop him one of these days, carting him about like you do. Up to you and down to Anna all day long!"

Gran did not know about the zoo in the attic. Nobody did.

Right at the beginning they had thought of telling Nathan, but the trouble with Nathan was that he could not keep a secret for one minute. Usually he would have found them out, anyway, but, luckily for Danny and Anna, he had other worries. Lately he was spending a great deal of time at Arun's house, studying the twins with a mixture of curiosity and horror.

Anna's family knew nothing about the zoo because they supposed she was upstairs playing with Danny, and Danny's mother suspected nothing at all. Danny and Anna did their zoo-keeping after school, before she got home, and at weekends when she was often out working. The Miss Kent sisters were regular customers on Saturday mornings and nobody from Paradise House (except Old McDonald) would have thought of going to a hairdresser's when Danny's mother could do them just as well at home. All this extra work made Danny's mother very busy and the only thing she noticed was that the swamp water had disappeared from under Danny's bed. She was very pleased indeed that it was gone and she did not ask where it was, in case it came back.

One day when Danny was alone in the attic, he noticed five black lumps hanging from a corner of the roof. He went down to the kitchen and borrowed the kitchen stool and climbed up and prodded them. One of the lumps moved. Danny poked again and the lump spread out a tiny, leathery half-umbrella of a wing. Danny fell backwards off the stool so hard that a crack appeared in his bedroom ceiling. When Anna came up she found him making a new notice.

Five wild
bats

said the notice.

"How wild?" asked Anna.

Danny pointed out the lumps hanging in the corner.

"They don't look wild at all," said Anna, half-relieved and half-disappointed. "They don't even look alive. They look as dead as my caterpillars. I like the birds best, after Oscar."

The sparrows were in and out constantly now, and one day a starling came with them, and the next day three more.

"Good," said Anna. "Birds are much more exciting than things in jars and lumps in corners and invisible rats and mice!"

"I don't think the rats and mice *are* invisible," said Danny. "I think they come out at night."

But Anna hoped very much that they were invisible and she made them a special sign to encourage them to stay that way. It read:

Invisible.
rats and mice
Do not disturb

Chapter Four

Tame
wild fox

After a while it seemed to Danny that he
had always been a zoo-keeper. He felt as if
he had always chopped up cabbage for the
pigeons and bread for the sparrows and
starlings. He grew quite expert in the trail-
ing of wandering snails and the handling of
Mr-Harper-In-The-Box (who bit). Wobbling
dangerously on the kitchen stool he had
admired and named the bats. He had been
delighted when he looked them up in his
animal books and discovered that, as well
as being a protected species, they could also
give a nasty bite. His zoo, though small,
contained rare and dangerous animals.

"My father saw a fox this morning," said
Anna, bouncing up the stairs to meet him
one day.

Danny stared at her.

"He said, 'Don't tell the world but do tell Danny.' He knew you'd be pleased."

"A fox?" asked Danny, and his heart jumped inside him and he knew that the thing he needed most in the world was a fox for his zoo.

"Walking down our road!"

"Walking down our road?"

"Very early this morning, on his way back from work."

"He was joking," said Danny.

"He wasn't."

"Perhaps it was a dog and he got mixed up."

"Of course he didn't."

"Or a cat. A ginger cat."

"Ask him yourself, then," said Anna, slightly crossly, so Danny did, and Anna's father confirmed that he really had seen a fox pattering down the road early that morning.

"Do you think it was a pet fox that had escaped?" asked Danny.

"It was a real wild fox, on its own, walking down the road," said Anna's father.

"There are foxes in London. I've seen them before. Don't talk about it too much though, Danny. Not everyone likes to have them around."

Danny sat through school that day in a daze and returned to the attic in the evening with a whirl of foxy dreams and schemes tumbling round his head.

"Hallo!" said Anna, who for once had arrived before him. She didn't mind being alone in the attic any more. She and Danny had moved so many tiles that it was now quite bright and cheerful. She was sitting in a patch of sunlight, polishing snails with cottonwool and butter, a lovely job that made them shine like new conkers.

"I've saved you three!" she told Danny.

"Three what?"

"Snails to polish."

"Thanks," said Danny absent-mindedly.

"There was a starling and four sparrows when I came in," Anna told him. "They just flew off as I came up the stairs."

"I wish they wouldn't," said Danny. "In

50

a proper zoo they'd have to stay."

"You mustn't tell anyone about that fox," warned Anna.

"I'm not daft," replied Danny, rubbing away at a snail, his mind full of questions. "I should like a fox."

"I should like an elephant," said Anna.

"I mean really, not just pretending."

"So do I," said Anna. "I would ride to school on it."

The mention of school made Danny wonder if Mr Harper would know the answers to some of his questions.

The next morning, in the middle of maths, he stuck up his hand and asked, "Mr Harper?"

"Yes?" said Mr Harper.

"Can you tame foxes?"

"Me?" asked Mr Harper. "I can't tame anything! I was savaged by a squirrel once!"

"Can some people, though?" asked Danny, ignoring Anna's glares from across the room.

"Tell me what you mean by tame," said

Mr Harper.

"Oh," said Danny. "Not biting, and coming when it's called and doing what I say."

"Why should it?" asked Anna, bouncing indignantly in her seat.

"Exactly my opinion," said Mr Harper. "I'm sure it's possible, Danny, but after all, why should it?"

Danny very nearly replied that it would have to if it was going to live in his attic, but luckily Arun saved him by remarking, "Our twins need taming. They bite. One of them bit Nathan!"

"They'll grow out of it," said Mr Harper comfortingly, "as Nathan gets older and tougher and less edible . . . Back to work everyone! What are you doing, Nathan?"

Nathan, who had been secretly struggling out of his trousers in order to show Craig his bite, hurriedly pulled them on again and the lesson resumed.

"You nearly told about my dad's fox!" said Anna accusingly as soon as she got Danny alone outside.

"'Course I didn't. I was only seeing if it would be possible."

"What would be possible?" asked Anna.

"The birds would be all right," continued Danny. "They'd fly off when it got too close. And I expect the rats and mice have plenty of places to escape to, and the bats would be quite safe . . . "

"Danny!" said Anna.

"We'd have to move the snails and the caterpillars and Mr-Harper-In-The-Box and the woodlice."

"Danny!" exploded Anna.

"It would be lovely company for Oscar!"

"It would eat Oscar!"

"Don't be silly. Oscar's a fish! He'd be safe in his bowl."

"It would drink the water and then eat Oscar! Anyway, it's an awful idea! You couldn't catch him. Poor fox if you did!"

"We could tame him," argued Danny. "And he'd have the whole attic to play in and plenty of food and he'd be nice and dry and we would look after him."

"It would be impossible," said Anna.

"We could call him Rufus," said Danny. "When he got used to us, we could take him for walks on a lead."

"Anyway, you would never catch him," said Anna. "How could you?"

"I don't know yet," said Danny. "Perhaps, when he got really tame, Mum would let him sleep on my bed at nights. It would be like having a dog, but a hundred times better."

Suddenly the zoo in the attic, which had been a lovely secret game, became frightening to Anna. She did not believe for one moment that Danny could catch the fox, but she knew quite well that if he could, he would. And he would make a new sign which read,

Tame
wild fox

Anna thought there should be no such thing as tame wild foxes.

"I hate your zoo!" she said suddenly. "You are cruel!"

Danny, who loved every member of it, down to the last hung-up caterpillar and invisible mouse, looked at her in disbelief.

"I wish I'd never given you Oscar now!" said Anna.

For one horrible moment Danny thought that he might start to cry. He squeezed both eyes together hard and when he opened them again, Anna had vanished.

That afternoon he could hardly bear to go home. He walked back to Paradise House as slowly as possible and stopped outside for a half-hearted game of football with Nathan. When Nathan scored his twentieth goal (to Danny's two) he gave up and went indoors.

There was no sign of Anna waiting in the hall for him. There was no answer when he knocked on her door. There was no one home in his own flat. He climbed the attic stairs to the zoo and there was no zoo.

Nothing was left. The boxes and jars were

gone. The notices were gone. The zoo kitchen had vanished and there were no birds. The zoo was an attic again, grey slates and grey cobwebs and grey, dusty boards. There was nothing left except Oscar, swimming round and round his bowl in the middle of the floor.

Chapter Five

Danny did what he always did in a crisis.
He crawled under his quilt and thought. So
that no ray of light might accidentally disturb the blackness of his thoughts, he
screwed his eyes tight shut and pushed his
face into the pillow. Straight away he made
up his mind that the only thing he could
possibly do was to stay in bed for ever.
When he had decided this, he curled himself
up into an uncomfortable lump and waited
to see what would happen next.

What happened next was that his mother
came home.

"Danny, tell me what's wrong!" she said
as soon as she discovered where he was, and
she reached down and hugged as much of
the lump on the bed as she could get her

arms around. This was difficult because Danny and the quilt were curled into a huge unfriendly hedgehog shape. Nothing showed outside except Danny's grubby trainers. They had made black streaks on the clean sheet.

"Nothing's the matter," muttered the hump in the bed.

"Do you feel ill? Have you hurt yourself?"

"No," said the hump.

"Are you in trouble at school?"

"No."

"What have you broken?" asked Danny's mother, suddenly remembering that Danny had taken to his bed the time he and Nathan had accidentally dropped the clock out of the window.

"Nothing," said the hump indignantly.

"Who have you quarrelled with, then?"

This time the hump did not reply, so Danny's mother knew that she had guessed correctly.

"Nathan?" she asked. "Arun? Robert or Craig?"

"No one that matters," said Danny.

"What are you crying for, then?"

"I'M NOT CRYING!" said Danny, suddenly shooting up from under the quilt. "I'm just fed up!"

"Oh?" said his mother.

"With stupid Anna."

"Anna!" exclaimed Danny's mother.

"However did you manage to quarrel with Anna?"

"I didn't. She quarrelled with me."

"I can't imagine Anna quarrelling with anyone," said Danny's mother crossly, because she had been so worried. "Look at those marks you've made on the sheet! Next time you go to bed in a huff, take your shoes off first!"

"It's all Anna's fault," said Danny, kicking off his trainers and getting back under the quilt.

"Your gran's right," said Danny's mother. "You *are* a dreadful sulker!"

This tactless and unmotherly remark did nothing to cheer Danny up and left him with no choice but to stay in bed all evening. He spent the first hour or so sulking and the next two or three feeling sorry for himself and inventing punishments for Anna and then, having refused to come out for supper, he began to feel hungry. Once he started to think about food he could not stop and, as soon as he thought his mother was safely in bed and asleep, he sneaked into

the little kitchen and made himself two
large cheese and pickle sandwiches. The
pickles were so strong they filled him with
courage. Perhaps he would not stay in bed

for ever, after all. Almost cheerfully he sawed off a lump of Gran's terrible, brick-like gingerbread (usually only eaten as a last resort) and took it back to bed with him.

Gnawing cautiously, Danny began to make plans for a new zoo. The birds would still come, and the rats and the mice. The bats would still be hanging under the roof and a fox really had been seen walking down the street. Oscar . . . But his mind skidded away from thinking about Oscar. He could easily collect more snails and beetles and insects. There were squirrels in the park that were practically tame already . . .

It was slow work, eating Gran's ginger-bread. Gran's eyes were not very good and she sometimes included nasty surprises in her baking by mistake. Danny quite often found milk bottle tops and matches and eggshells and once (horribly) a Brillo pad. It was quite a triumph to finish a piece unwounded. Danny couldn't remember when he ever had before.

Perhaps it means good luck to the new zoo, he thought drowsily, and fell asleep.

*   *   *

That night Danny dreamed about zoos. In his dream he was in a zoo. He was in a cage and the animals were watching him.

I must wake up, thought Danny in his sleep and with enormous effort he managed to drag open his eyes. It made no difference. He was still asleep and the animals were still watching him. Dozens and dozens of animals. Hundreds of eyes peering in at him.

I've got to escape! thought Danny frantically and began to turn and turn in his cage, but there was no corner to hide in that was not full of gazing animals. He reached for the window and saw bars.

Usually dreams are silent but this one wasn't. The animals that surrounded Danny were not just watching him. They were also roaring, howling, flapping and thudding.

"Let me out!" screamed Danny. "Let me out! Let me out!" And this time he really did wake up. The animals became just wallpaper animals and the window became his ordinary old-fashioned window with the familiar nursery bars. The bedroom light was switched on and his mother was hugging him. Danny stopped screaming but the animals did not stop roaring.

"If this carries on much longer the roof will blow off!" said Danny's mother. "I've never known such a wind!"

"Wind?" asked Danny, listening in amazement to the roars and howls above his head.

"What did you think it was?"

"I dreamed it was animals roaring at me!"

"Serves you right for stuffing yourself

with cheese and pickle sandwiches in the middle of the night," said his mother. "It would give anyone nightmares!"

She laughed at Danny's surprised face and then the laugh turned into a squeal as something very heavy thudded on the ceiling above Danny's bed. The crack that had appeared when Danny first fell off the stool in the attic grew suddenly blacker and wider and a trickle of plaster dust came pouring down.

"That was a tile!" exclaimed Danny's mother. "Good grief! Listen to that!"

There was a huge clattering, skating sound and a moment later a loud smash as

it landed in the garden outside. Danny and his mother ran to unlock the attic door, pulled it open and looked up into the dark. They found themselves staring at the sky and a bright moon shining through a foam of racing clouds. There was an enormous hole in the roof.

"Oscar! Oscar! Oscar!" screamed Danny and started running up the attic stairs. A moment later he came crashing down them again, as his mother rugby-tackled his ankles and dragged him back.

"Oscar's up there!" he shouted, struggling to escape her grip.

"Don't be so stupid, Danny!" shouted his mother. "What are you thinking of? Oscar's probably tucked up safe with Anna!"

"He's not," said Danny. "He's up in the attic! We left him there!"

Chapter Six

The gale was blowing through the hole in the roof and down the attic stairs, tearing off tiles as it went. When Danny's mother slammed the door shut, the wind still blew into the attic but now it could not get out.

Bump! Bump! Bump! went the roof of Paradise House, rising and falling as the wind tried to escape.

"Oscar! Oscar! Oscar!" wailed Danny.

I am having a terrible dream! thought Danny's mother as she leaned on the door and clutched her ears against the noise. And in my terrible dream I go up into the attic (which is full of spiders) to rescue a goldfish because the roof might blow off. And telling herself that hopefully she would probably soon wake up, she pulled open the door, climbed the attic stairs,

seized Oscar from the middle of the floor and, dodging broken tiles and plaster and flying cobwebs and spiders, scuttled as quickly as she could back down again.

A few moments later Paradise House was wide awake. The grown-ups were hurrying up and down the stairs, exploring the damage, exclaiming at the mess outside, and telling each other that it was more than time they had a new roof.

"Better it came off in the summer than in the winter, anyway," said Anna's father cheerfully. "And it's nearly over! It's blown itself out already."

The wind was dying as quickly as it had arisen. Outside, the street was calm and nearly quiet. People suddenly found there was no need to shout. It was almost morning.

Upstairs in Anna's bedroom, Danny and Anna sat exhausted with excitement and relief, clutching Oscar in his goldfish bowl.

"Your mum's a hero," said Anna. "All that wind! All those tiles smashing down . . . "

71

"All those spiders!" said Danny. "That's what she minded most!"

"Didn't she ask what Oscar was doing in the attic?"

"No," said Danny. "I tried to explain but she put her hands over her ears and said, 'Please don't tell me! Please don't tell me! Do you know how much a new roof will cost?'"

"Oh," said Anna.

"So I shut up," said Danny.

"Doesn't she know about the zoo?"

"No. Nobody does except me and you and Oscar."

"I wonder if your mother thinks the tiles came off because of us," said Anna. "I suppose we did move them about a bit."

"We made holes," said Danny bluntly.

"Oh well," said Anna comfortably. "Old McDonald told Dad that he's been saying for years that Paradise House needed a new roof, and this has proved he was right. I was there when they were talking. You could see Old McDonald was quite pleased."

"It definitely needs a new roof now,

72

anyway!" said Danny.

It was light enough now to see quite clearly. Anna went back to the window to stare in fascinated horror at the piles of broken tiles scattered in the garden.

"Fancy all that mess just because of a few little holes," she remarked. "Good job I let all the animals go! If I hadn't, the whole zoo would have blown away."

"I suppose it would," said Danny. "What did you do with them?"

"I put them all back where we got them from. I didn't touch the bats, but they flew off themselves when I was shooing away a pigeon that didn't want to go."

Danny waited for a minute to see if she was going to apologize, but she did not.

"You're not to go and get them back," she told him.

"I don't want to," replied Danny.

"I've decided I like animals much better outside."

"So do I," agreed Danny, remembering his dream.

"Even foxes?" asked Anna, turning from

the window to look at him, her eyes shining with excitement.

"Especially foxes," Danny told her.

"Come and look here, then!" said Anna eagerly. "There! Running along by that wall!"

Together they stood and gazed in delight as the fox came nearer. It flickered like a flame beside hedges and walls, golden red

in the sunlight and a dusky gleam in the shadows. Sometimes it darted into gateways and openings but reappeared, each time a little closer, so that soon Anna and Danny could clearly see the thick, soft fur and dark, pointed ears.

The bedroom door opened gently and Anna's father came in.

"Look out of the win . . . " he began. "Oh! You're there! Isn't it beautiful!"

Even before they could agree the door opened again.

"Here they are!" whispered Anna's mother.

"Quick!" said Danny's mother, following behind. "Quick! Both of you . . . Oh, you've spotted it!"

"Yes," said Anna.

A moment later there was a knock and the Miss Kents came in.

"We thought Danny must be here," they said. "You'll never guess what the caretaker showed us a moment . . . Oh good! You've seen!"

"Thank you for coming to tell me," said

Danny, making room so that they could look too. "Hello, Nathan!" he added, as Nathan burst panting into the room.

"Dad said to tell you there's . . . Are you looking at it already? Is it a real fox? Let me see before it goes!"

"Quick then!" said Danny. "He's just coming into the garden."

The fox crossed the garden and disappeared from sight and a sigh went up from the people at the window.

"Gone!" said Anna, and the spell was broken. Everyone suddenly remembered that they were not dressed or washed or brushed and that the roof had blown off in the night. Nathan, discovering to his horror that he was wearing his mother's pink dressing gown, vanished as quickly as he could. The Miss Kents caught sight of each other's steel curlers and hurried bashfully away. Anna's parents went up with Danny's mother to view the damage and remove any stray spiders that might have been blown downstairs. Danny and Anna were left alone. They looked at each other, and they looked at Oscar, the innocent cause of all the night's excitements. Voices from all over the house were asking the same question,

"However could it have happened? However *could* it have happened?"

"Wasn't it windy?" asked Anna politely, and her eyes said, "I will never tell!"

"Yes, wasn't it," agreed Danny just as carefully polite, and nodded to show that he understood.

If you enjoyed reading *The Zoo in the Attic*, you might also like the other 'Paradise House' stories by Hilary McKay.

Danny, Anna and Nathan continue their adventures in *The Treasure in the Garden*, *The Echo in the Chimney* and *The Magic in the Mirror*